I'M A BAKED POTATO!

chronicle books · san francisco

By Elise Primavera

Art by Juana Medina

There was a lady who loved baked potatoes.
She ate one every day. She even had a potato garden
in her backyard because she hated to run out.

The lady also loved dogs, and so
one day she went and got one.

She chose him because he seemed to
fit so nicely in her arms.

"You remind me of something," she said to the dog.
"What could it be?"

The dog was smooth.
The dog was warm.
She could have eaten him
right up.

"That's exactly it!" she exclaimed.
"You're just like a baked potato!"

And that was what she told him first thing every morning. "You're my little baked potato."

Throughout the day she called for him. "Here, Baked Potato!"

Or commanded, "Roll over, Baked Potato!"

And so on.

The lady was an excellent pet owner.

She and the dog ate all their meals together by the fire.

She let him sleep under the covers.
She loved the dog even more than she
loved baked potatoes.

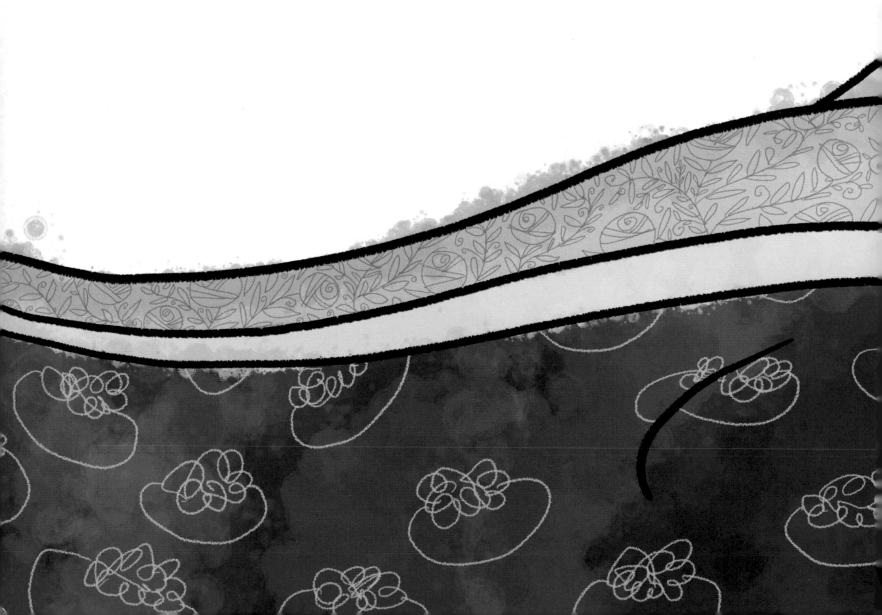

Then one day the lady
went out.

The dog went out, too.

"Where's the lady?" he wondered.

He walked down the driveway.
He looked everywhere for her.

He walked farther and farther.
Where was the lady?

He came to a
small house.

A big dog ran to him and barked nastily.
"Who are you?" he snarled.

"I'm a baked potato," the dog replied.

"You look more like a groundhog to me!
Go away before I bite you!"

The dog had never heard such yelling.

"Do you know where the lady is?"

But the big dog just shouted, "Scram!"

The dog wandered farther down the street.
He looked all around.
Was she around the corner?
Was she over the next hill?

"Where's the lady?"

The sky became dark. The air became cold.
The dog became worried.

It began to rain.

The dog thought of how it felt to be held in the lady's arms.
He thought of how right now they'd be sharing a meal together by the fire.
He thought of the bed where she let him sleep under the covers.

"The lady!" he called. "Where are you?"

A fox heard his plaintive cry. "Who are you?"

"I'm a . . . groundhog?" The dog had never been so upset.

"You look more like a nice plump bunny rabbit to me."
The fox licked his lips. "I just love bunny rabbit."

"What a relief," said the dog.

"Come with me," said the fox.
He led the dog to his creepy house.

The fox turned on his oven. "You would be good with carrots and onions," he muttered.

"Who are Carrots and Onions?" the dog asked. "Do they know where the lady is?"

The fox had a devilish grin. "We'll ask them, shall we?"

Just then a voice said,
"What do you think you're doing?"

Right at the fox's door stood an old owl.
The owl shook his head at the fox (who he
knew to be a coward).

"Who are you?" the owl asked the dog.

"I guess I'm a bunny rabbit," the dog said,
his lips trembling.

The owl gave the fox a dirty look. "Come with me."
Then he took the dog by the paw and brought him
to his cheerful house.

He looked into the dog's eyes. "You are not a bunny rabbit."

"So I'm a groundhog?" The dog had never been so confused.

The owl shook his head. "I don't think so."

"I knew it," the dog said. "I'm a baked potato."

"You are a dog," said the owl.

Bing! The timer on the owl's oven sounded.

"*This* is a baked potato."

The dog sniffed it. It smelled like the lady.

The dog was taken aback.
"You seem to know a lot," he said.
"Do you know where the lady is?"

"I don't know that," the owl said. "But I do know that
dogs are very good at finding things, especially
with their noses."

"Like the lady?" the dog asked hopefully.

"Like the lady," the owl replied firmly.

Outside the dog took the owl's advice.
He sniffed and smelled the lady. The smell
wafted on the breeze.

He followed it away from the cheerful house,
past the creepy house, and past the small house,
then around the corner and down the street.

Soon he could hear her calling, "Baked Potato! Baked Potato!"

Sure enough standing in the porch light was the lady.

He jumped into her arms and she
showered him with kisses.

"My little baked potato,"
she cooed, squeezing him tight.
"I should have known you'd like
walks in the rain—you're
just like me!"

It was good to be back, but the dog would never be the same. He knew he was not a baked potato, or a groundhog, or a bunny rabbit.

He knew exactly what he was.

"I'm just like me."

For Lulu, who will always be
my little baked potato! —E.P.

To Cata & Mauricio. —J.M.

Library of Congress Cataloging-in-Publication
Data available.

ISBN 978-1-4521-5592-0

Manufactured in China.

FSC
www.fsc.org
MIX
Paper from
responsible sources
FSC™ C104723

Design by Amelia Mack.
Typeset in Cochin.
The illustrations in this book were created digitally, using Procreate.

10 9 8 7 6 5 4 3 2 1

Chronicle Books LLC
680 Second Street
San Francisco, California 94107
www.chroniclekids.com